# The House of Wynne Lift

## Cheryl Peña

This is a work of fiction. Names, characters, places, and incidents are products of the author's imagination or are used fictitiously and are not to be construed as real. Any resemblance to actual events, locations, organizations, or persons, living or dead, is entirely coincidental.

**World Castle Publishing, LLC**
Pensacola, Florida
Copyright © Cheryl Peña 2021
KDP ISBN: 9798537311096
Paperback ISBN: 9781955086530
eBook ISBN: 9781955086547
First Edition World Castle Publishing, LLC, August 2, 2021
http://www.worldcastlepublishing.com

Cover: Karen Fuller

Editor: Maxine Bringenberg

# CHAPTER 1

The journey had been long and arduous for the researcher and his companion, a reporter he had met in New York. The long plane ride had seemed bad enough, but the trip through the rough land and eerie mountains drained them. They came around through what they deduced was a dried river bed and clambered up the bank to stand by a scraggly-looking tree in the midst of a desolate area.

"There it is," the researcher announced. "The Castle Tower."

He pointed to the top of an

outcropping on a mountain that seemed to have battlements surrounding the blunted peak and spires collected at the foot of the hill. It appeared strangely bizarre against the graying sky, and the reporter sensed that something was about to happen besides the imminent rain.

"The house of Wynne Lift," the researcher finished after a pause.

"Who is this mysterious Wynne Lift?" the reporter asked.

"Ah, Mr. Wylie! What we know is that he was a wealthy recluse living in London, but he left society to live here. No one has ever been inside, and it *has* been nearly twenty years."

Wylie let out his breath in exhaustion and perhaps a little from frustration at not getting his question answered completely. Silence was around them, but he sensed the drama of the moment as his eyes focused on the top of the tower. It was amazing. He couldn't imagine a person wanting to live in a cave for twenty years.

"How do we know anyone is still up there? No one has ever seen him. How do we know he's not dead?"

"Oh, no. Wynne Lift is alive. These are not rumors. This is not folklore. We know he was a very wealthy, private man, but it shocked the city to learn of his plan to leave civilization. 'Why would a man of his stature want to live like a savage?' was the question everyone asked. But travelers in this area all claim to hear violins play when they pass the mountains...and Wynne Lift was an exceptional violinist. Do not tell me you think he is dead."

"These are stories...people who have been trekking for days in the wilderness. They're weary...they're hearing things. It could all be just overactive imaginations."

The researcher was perturbed by Wylie's skepticism. "I've heard them. Don't tell *me* I have an overactive imagination. I know what I heard is real. Believe me, you have not wasted your trip. We *will* meet Wynne Lift."

The very name sent shivers over Wylie's body as he looked up at the sky and then at their destination: The Castle Tower.

~*~

The rocks were rough on their feet, and they had nearly become faint from exertion as they neared the top of the mountain. Wylie felt his foot slide on a loose rock, but he was too slow in reacting. He grabbed the first thing his hands touched as he went down, finally able to grasp what was happening in his tired mind. He didn't even have the strength to call out, but his traveling companion had heard him and was there immediately to pull him up. Wylie was disoriented for a couple of minutes before he gestured that he was all right, and they continued to climb.

Slowly they neared the outcropping and sidestepped until they could finally walk out onto it. The "battlements" on the tower now resembled the points on a crown. Somehow, Wylie knew this discovery would be nothing like he expected. The sky seemed to almost yellow with the redness of the rock. Wylie was surprised at how the color was not apparent from the ground as it was silhouetted, even against a clouded sky. He knew this wouldn't be the only surprise. Watching in his nervousness, he observed the researcher examining the stone formations in front of them. Wylie took this opportunity to take a few photographs. Then it occurred to him what the researcher was doing.

"Professor Livingston? You looking for the entrance?"

"Yes. Yes, indeed I am. I know he would have hidden it. Wouldn't want others to bother him, you know?"

"I know." He thought a moment. "Wouldn't he try to put it where it would be difficult to get to? Maybe on the side or out front?"

The professor agreed. Both of them walked around to one side, passing one large mass of rock and then slipping into a crevice between it and the next battlement.

A shiny object caught Livingston's eye. "Well, that wasn't hidden well at all!"

"What?" Wylie spun around. Before him was a door with an entrance carved out of the rock. "A door?" He took a photograph out of habit.

"I rather expected a boulder to push in. A door to a cave! Extraordinary! This is going to be a spectacular visit. I told you that you wouldn't be disappointed." Livingston seemed overjoyed. "Now, remember what I told you. Don't seem too excited. Remain calm and quiet. This man hasn't seen civilization or another human being in twenty years. No sudden movements. We don't want to frighten him. Just have a chat."

"I got it. I'll be careful." Wylie was getting more than just a little annoyed. He tried to attribute it to fatigue and took a deep breath to relax.

"Right. Well, let's cut to the chase. No formalities, eh?" Livingston raised his hand and gave a knock on the door.

There were a few moments of silence before he knocked again. Wylie regained his skepticism. "He's not there.

We've wasted our time. Let's set up a camp or something and rest before heading home."

Livingston grabbed the arm of the retreating man. "Wait a moment—"

"No, he's not there. Give it up. You were wrong. It happens."

Livingston knocked again. "Please. It can't hurt to try, even if no one answers."

"No, just knocking on an abandoned house gives me the creeps. Let's *go*!"

Suddenly the doorknob turned, and the door moved slowly and cautiously open. "Who's there?" a quiet voice asked from the other side. The speaker did not make himself visible.

Both Livingston and Wylie were astonished. "Wynne Lift?"

"Yes. Who are *you*?"

"I'm Professor Foster Livingston, and this is Peter Wylie, a reporter from New York. We were hoping you'd allow us to chat with you for a few moments."

"Do you want to write an article about me?"

Wylie answered. "With your permission, of course, sir."

"Well, I'm not sure I want to be in the news anymore. I'll be glad to let you in for a visit since you've gone through all the trouble to get here. I know you need to rest. We can chat all you like, but I'm afraid I'd have to consider the issue of an article for a while before making a decision. I'm just not too excited about that prospect at the moment. But, please come in." The door opened wider, and the two strangers walked inside, finding themselves atop a narrow stairway, which Wynne Lift was already heading down. "Close the door behind you."

All Wylie could see following their mysterious host was a velvety smoking jacket worn by a man with silvery-gray hair. His dark pants blended into the darkness of the corridor.

Soon they came to another door, and when it opened, light filled the stairwell and Wynne Lift disappeared into another room. As both men reached the bottom of the stairs, they saw a Persian rug lying near the door on what was otherwise a marble tile floor. It was almost a contradiction as they entered. The tile floor, the expensive furniture, the gold, the works of art...everything a civilized home would have, set off by rock walls and ceiling. It wasn't the "cave" they imagined.

"Here, have a seat. You must be exhausted."

Both men sat on a lovely Queen Anne sofa, getting their first glimpse of Lift's face. It was perfectly shaved, and the skin looked very healthy, although pale. He had a very kind smile and kind blue eyes that sparkled in the dim light.

"Thank you, sir. We really appreciate your generosity. We would have given you prior notice instead of dropping in uninvited like this, but we didn't really know how to contact you, and we didn't think you'd let us in if you knew we were coming." Wylie gave an unsure laugh.

"Probably not. You're very wise." The smile still hadn't faded.

"Well, you're being very polite to us after we did this, came unexpectedly. I know you'd probably rather be alone, but—"

"No, don't bother. It's quite all right. It's rather nice to speak to someone after so long a time. I should think it a chance to explain everything and to hear what's been happening on the outside."

Livingston remarked, "You haven't seen sunlight in twenty years? I can't imagine!"

"No, no. I don't stay locked up. This isn't a dungeon. This is my home. I sometimes go out and play my violin in the moonlight. Sometimes I stay until sunrise or go out at sunset. But otherwise, the light is much too bright for me."

"I'm really anxious to hear your story, Mr. Lift."

"Later. First, you need to rest. Enjoy yourselves. I'll show you to your rooms." They stood to follow Lift. "You know, when I first started building this place, I intended on taking my family with me." His laugh showed a little resentment. "But when I was finally ready to go, none of them wanted to come. Now I finally have use for those extra rooms! They're furnished, of course. I suppose I was waiting for one of them to change their minds. Foolish, isn't it?"

"No, sir —"

Wylie was interrupted by an elbow to his side from Livingston. When he looked back at Lift, he noticed the man was paying no attention to them. Both stood respectfully silent.

"Anyway," Lift burst out suddenly, "I need to show you where you'll be staying. I'm sorry, gentlemen."

"Perfectly all right, sir," Wylie acknowledged politely, taking a second to glare back at Livingston before falling in step behind Lift toward an arched doorway leading into a corridor with built-in light fixtures. The hall was just to the right of the door from which they'd entered, yet somehow Wylie could not imagine going back up that flight of stairs into the sun again.

# CHAPTER 2

When Wylie opened his eyes, he was unsure of whether it was night or morning. He wasn't even sure how long he'd been asleep. The past few days had been particularly draining and left him feeling completely bewildered. All he could remember were the many nights he'd spent under the stars in the wilderness, and now here he was lying on a mattress with feather pillows. Their brief encounter with the elusive figure of Wynne Lift made little of an impression on him except that, even after seeing and speaking with the man, he still did not know one thing about him. The details slowly came back to him...the treacherous climb, the not-so-hidden door, the smoking jacket and silver hair, the marble tile and plush décor. What would he discover today? He was reluctant to leave the room, feeling extremely uncomfortable in a stranger's place of residence. Suddenly his natural desire for knowledge was stilled, and he could understand sincerely why so many people disliked reporters. He felt their presence was an intrusion and that Livingston and he were an unnecessary burden on their more-than-gracious host.

A knock came unexpectedly at the door, and he was completely unprepared for it. "Just a minute," he said, before hastily dressing in the robe provided by Lift and quickly running his fingers through his hair a few times. "I'm coming," he reiterated upon hearing another knock, and reached the door a little out of breath. "Yes?"

The gentleman's face beamed in the opening. "Good morning, Mr. Wylie. I'm serving breakfast in a few minutes if you and your friend would like to join me. You have time to shave, wash, dress, and whatever else you need to do. I hope you like lots of French food!"

"Of course, sir. Thank you, sir. That's very generous of you, sir," he overcompensated.

"Yes, yes, well...I'll see you in a few minutes, then. Cheerio!"

The man smiled broadly before retreating down the hallway, back in the direction of the kitchen — or so Wylie supposed. He really had no idea where the breakfast room was or even if one existed. Maybe they would eat in the living room by the coffee table? Maybe Professor Livingston would come to knock on his door first, and he'd use the excuse that he was just following the professor should they get lost. Or maybe he should just make an educated guess.

~*~

Wynne Lift had cleared the table and served a light fruit salad for dessert, along with the stereotypical glass of juice. Livingston ate quickly with a voracious appetite and was sipping at the juices left at the bottom with his spoon, while Wylie, seated across from the professor, picked at it delicately with a fork.

"Quite amusing," Lift observed. "I would have thought the professor to have better manners than a New York reporter, but it's the other way 'round!"

Both men looked up, startled. "Excuse me, sir?" Wylie ventured.

Lift sat up abruptly. "I'm sorry. I apologize for my poor etiquette. You remember, gentlemen, I haven't had much chance to practice!"

"Of course, sir. I understand."

"You just don't match my expectations."

Wylie wasn't sure how to proceed but became somewhat brave. "Well, I can't speak for the professor, but I have lots of lunch meetings with people for business. I don't think I'm exceptionally polite. I just have to conduct myself in a certain manner in the circles I'm in. I'm led to believe the professor is unconventional anyway, so he's eccentric even when he's teaching. I don't know him personally, however. We met a few weeks ago."

Lift nodded. "I suppose I hadn't thought of that…it's been a while."

"Thank you also, Mr. Wylie, for your flattering description of my life," Livingston grunted.

"Sorry."

"Nonsense. He cleared up a

misconception. It wasn't taken to be derogatory," Lift defended.

Wylie felt bad anyway. "I'm sorry. I didn't mean to offend you. I only intended on making a point. I hadn't meant it that way."

Livingston still sulked, and his face twisted into a mass of wrinkles as he frowned.

"Let it go, Mr. Wylie. Really, I *am* interested in hearing about things. Have you...*do* you know about...my family? My...wife?"

"Uh...well, I...I don't really.... You lived in England still, didn't you?"

"Yes. Yes, I did. Are they still there?" Lift sounded impatient.

Wylie felt uneasy, not sure why he was so afraid of upsetting the old man who'd shown nothing but kindness since they'd arrived. "Yes, sir. All I know is what Professor Livingston told me.

I wasn't familiar with you, but I was intrigued by your story. If you do the interview, I would contact them to get their side of the story. I didn't want to bother them for no reason, so I thought I'd wait until after I'd talked to you."

The man looked as though he were hiding anger or trying not to let on that he felt insulted. "What stories *are* going 'round? You heard *those*?"

Wylie shifted self-consciously and cleared his throat nervously. "Um…well, not much. They're…no one knew much about you, sir. You were well-known as being wealthy. They wondered why you left…why you'd come *here*. There were speculations, but nothing out of the ordinary, I don't think. Then there were stories of travelers hearing violins out in this area, and it all came back from a twenty-year hiatus."

"Professor, what did you hear? I'm

sure you know more about occurrences in England than this *American!*"

Livingston was slightly perplexed at the sudden change in behavior. "Not much more on this story, I'm afraid," he answered anyway, trying to be somewhat diplomatic despite his previous insult from the reporter. "They thought you were antisocial or had a troubled relationship. Others thought you were tired of civilization. But after a time, the talk stopped...until the travelers began to speak up. Some called the tales rumors... and everyone speculated on whether you were alive or dead and what state you'd be in if you were alive. No one would have expected *this*."

Lift laughed at once. "Wonderful! It's such a funny thing! What else would they think? Why would I just go and live in a primitive cave with no conveniences at all? I hadn't gone mad!" His laughter reduced to chuckling, and he took a deep breath. "Is that what brought you two here?"

Wylie interrupted Livingston. "We wanted to know if the stories were true… what was the real truth. Rumors become extremely distorted along the way. I couldn't believe a story about a man who'd been away from human contact for twenty years. It was intriguing."

"Not to mention all the newspapers to be sold, right, Mr. Wylie?" Luckily, a grin accompanied the comment.

"Yes, to be honest, Mr. Lift. You are correct," Wylie said, without mentioning that there really weren't many newspapers anymore. "But I didn't really expect to find anything, so if I don't get the interview, sir, I won't be disappointed."

"I appreciate that."

"Also, under the circumstances,

I know you value your privacy, so I won't attempt to get anything published without your consent, as I'd said earlier."

"Splendid. But I really haven't decided for or against the interview yet. It's still early. Why don't you gentlemen stay for a while? I'll give you a tour! There's no rush, is there? I haven't even had time to think!"

The two guests looked at each other, contemplating, wondering what the other was thinking. But upon seeing each of their facial expressions, it was obvious they both agreed. "Offer accepted!" and "Why not?" resounded simultaneously.

"Wonderful!" Lift exclaimed.

# CHAPTER 3

The house was actually a subterranean mansion worthy of the most extravagant movie star. There were crystal chandeliers in the main rooms along with rich carpeting everywhere but those larger rooms. There were aeroponics bays with herbs and vegetables, a gym and a jogging track, a heated pool, a generator room — they still hadn't figured out what type of fuel was used — the list went on. Lift seemed extraordinarily proud of his achievement as if he himself had built it instead of designing it. He seemed to have thought of everything except how to get his family to come along. However, he was doing his best to make Livingston and Wylie feel welcome. He even offered to let them use all of the facilities at their leisure. Then he excused himself without explanation and gestured for them to continue exploring as he turned around. He seemed typically jovial as he left them, using a small monorail car he'd neglected to tell them about. Surprisingly, neither guest had even noticed the track that ran along the corridors.

"Either he doesn't want us using that, or there was so much to say that he forgot some things," Wylie proposed.

Livingston was perpetually criticizing his companion and now was no exception. "I'm sure some things would slip his mind. If you used the car every day and got used to it, you wouldn't think to mention it either. What's the matter with you? You switch places. You pretend to be friendly when he's around, and then you make rude comments behind his back. I'd hate to think what you'd say about me if I weren't here. Don't you have any friends?"

"Yes, I do. I don't think that was necessary, Professor. I wasn't trying to be rude. I only wondered why he didn't bring it up. You don't have to be so... rude just because I'm from New York and you're from London. It doesn't make you a better person or anything. You've been on my case since this trip began, treating me like an uncultured slob. Maybe my culture's different than yours, but that doesn't make me any less refined. Our standards are different because our background is different. *Different*. That's all. You misunderstood."

"Whoever said I didn't like Americans? I said *you* were rude."

"Shouldn't come from someone

Wynne Lift himself criticized."

Livingston's lips pursed together. "And when did he do that?"

Wylie shrugged. "When you made a fool of yourself by acting like *I* was rude...talking about eating habits or something."

Again, the researcher's lips pressed hard against each other in his anger. He couldn't immediately think of a response, but he definitely had plenty of things to say. It took a few seconds as his jaw shifted from side to side, grinding his teeth, then he let out his breath. "I don't know why I could have thought to bring you along with me. You have absolutely no manners, and I don't care what Wynne Lift said. Your statement was unflattering...Lift even considers himself a poor judge of etiquette. How would he know you were really a savage? He's had no practice whatsoever."

"I'll tell him you said that," Wylie retorted calmly. But that was what he said. Inside, his feelings were much less friendly towards their host. His flattery and polite "thank yous" and "sirs" were a mask for his discomfort. He didn't quite know the reason for his mistrust—there was no concrete answer. But his intuition told him something was wrong. It wasn't like Lift was hiding something, but more like there was something he should know. Only this time, his reporter's instinct told him to go home...no questions asked.

~*~

A small desk lamp burned brightly in the otherwise dark room. An e-book lay in front of him, but his heart was not into reading it. Instead, he stared at the rock wall against which the desk was positioned and imagined a window where he could see the stars. He never realized how much windows contributed to the lighting of a place. His sense of timing was completely lost, but he was sure it had to be nighttime because, although his watch was still set to New York time, he could still determine the hour through simple mathematics. He wondered how Lift could live like that. The atmosphere was becoming increasingly more oppressive the longer he stayed. Claustrophobia had never plagued him before, but he felt confined and cramped, as if in a cage. Yet still, Livingston wanted his research, interview, or whatever.

Wylie had to admit, he had been very interested prior to their arrival, but now all he could think of was what it would be like to see the sky again. How Livingston could stand it and keep sight of his objective was beyond him. He was about to climb the walls. Still, another question that troubled him was how Lift could control them without ever placing restrictions on either of them. Was it just his own paranoia that prevented him from asking questions, walking around freely, using the facilities, or just walking out the door? Did Livingston feel similarly, or was he alone? He was even afraid to write down his concerns for fear that Lift would find the papers and read them. He was afraid to speak quietly to himself about it for fear that Lift could somehow hear him through some sort of Orwell-esque surveillance. What then? Did he really believe Lift had authority over them now? What could possibly happen? Lift had as yet to show them his real angry side.

Wylie turned in his chair to look around the room. The feeble light from the desk was barely enough to highlight the edges of the furniture. His own shadow fell across the floor in an oddly-shaped manner from the obstacles of the bed, nightstand, and other clutter. Every movement he made created an echoing sensation, but he was cut off from all outside noise. It was a serene setting, one he would have enjoyed had he been into his reading, working on an important report or story for work, or even finishing his income tax forms. But at that moment, he wanted noise. He wanted contact with someone else. He wanted to hear crickets and traffic and the neighbors arguing next door. He sighed. Even the silence seemed to echo. He felt as though a radio had been on since the day he was born and had only just been switched off for the first time. He had never been anywhere that quiet in all his life. It was definitely a new experience.

A sudden knock reverberated through the rock chamber, disturbing his thoughts. He abruptly realized that perhaps he did want to be left alone with his silly preoccupations but stood anyway. Wynne Lift didn't have to know about his worries, did he? Wylie took a deep breath before reluctantly going to the door and opening it. But, instead of the sparkling blue eyes and silver hair he'd expected to see, the professor's face awaited him from the hall.

"Professor?" he said, surprised.

"May I speak with you for a few moments?" The man actually looked troubled.

"Sure." He stepped aside to allow his visitor to pass, then closed the door. "What's the matter?"

Livingston looked around a little, noting the similarities between Wylie's room and his own. Finally seeming satisfied, he sat on the edge of the bed and watched Wylie take the chair at the desk before he felt settled enough to attempt a discussion. "I, er, don't know how to say this...." He looked around again, hoping a distraction could give him a change of topic. None came. He cleared his throat nervously. "I feel strange...." He glanced around as if someone would suddenly be there watching. "I can't sleep. Last night was easy enough; I was exhausted. But we've rested, and now I keep *thinking*. I feel all the kilos of the earth on top of us. It feels like it'll all collapse, and we'll all be crushed."

"You're claustrophobic?" He was genuinely surprised and felt true sympathy. It was bad enough for him, but he couldn't imagine the discomfort of a true claustrophobic. After all, it wasn't a natural cave; it was man-made. He tended to trust nature to create things that would last thousands of years rather than a human being—although humans did have nuclear waste to their credit.

The professor shrugged. "I didn't

think so before, but I've had episodes in the past."

"It's not just you," Wylie confided, still fearing the microphones he'd created in his mind. "I have been a bit nervous, actually. I guess that's why we never decided to do something like this, eh? Move out to the wilderness." He tried to make it a joke but didn't succeed.

"This is very different for me. Ordinarily, I'd love this whole thing. This is the kind of experience I usually thrive on...the unexpected, discovering places and learning about people. But even though I'm finding this very interesting, I can't help feeling uneasy." He sighed. "I don't know. Maybe I'm overreacting. Maybe it's just because this is the first chance I've had to think about all of this. I may, in a day or so, feel more relaxed... right?"

"I don't know. Maybe. Maybe I

will, too." He gave a smile that showed obvious doubt. "I hope so." He also hoped there were no cameras, but then he didn't know how advanced technology was twenty years ago...*Candid Camera* could do it, though.

"Maybe it's nothing. I should just go and try to get some sleep. Sorry to trouble you." He stood, suddenly resolving to be his usual assertive self.

"No trouble. I don't mind. Good night."

"Right. See you in the morning, then. Good night." He walked briskly to the door and almost let himself out but stopped, thinking it could be taken rudely, and waited for Wylie.

"Good night," Wylie repeated, receiving a nod from the professor to reciprocate, and he was alone once more, wanting very much to be a brave man but feeling more than anything else like he was only a child.

# Chapter 4

Wylie sauntered through the house, quietly noting to himself how big everything was, the amount of space. Only a few small lights were on, casting many shadows in the semi-darkness. But it would be a couple of hours before anyone else awoke, and he could not sleep. He knew something was wrong. He was never one plagued by insomnia, even after reporting a story that was particularly troubling. He was a hard worker and always fell asleep within minutes of reaching his bed, wherever that may be. He'd slept through scandals,

mass murders, terrorist attacks, and civil
unrest. But this was different. Nothing
had happened. As yet, he had no story
and only paranoid jitters after spending
too long down in a dark cave. What was
he so afraid of? *Was* it fear? He wasn't
even sure of that.

Instinctively he was drawn to the
Queen Anne where the professor and he
had sat upon their arrival and started for
it but stopped. There were many things
he hadn't even looked at, details not gone
over in the tour. On the wall to the right of
the door was a set of shelves with crystal
ornaments on it, some frosted glass, and
some cobalt blue decorative glasses also.
They sparkled like diamonds in the dim
light, a temptation he could not resist.
Curiosity pulled him closer, slowly, until
he was only inches away and gazing
upon the pieces as if he had never seen
such works before. But he *had,* and it

seemed like years ago.

He picked up a perfect blue sphere, turned it over in his hands, and then placed it carefully back in its designated spot. The figures were each unique, in flowing, abstract forms. He didn't know why, but it seemed somehow that they were all related, conveying some sort of vague message, but he couldn't figure it out, and he felt troubled. Water. That was the only connection he could see, and it was only an emotional reaction. They all reminded him of the sea. But *was* there a connection? *I'm being paranoid again*, he rationalized and turned himself away from the shelves. But as he walked away along the wall, he became engrossed in the rock itself.

He could see where people had worked at it, carving it roughly and quickly and leaving edges as if done in a hurry, which didn't surprise him, considering how much work was to be done. He rubbed his hand along it as he walked, almost feeling the pain of the men who must have put in long hard days and nights to complete the project on schedule. How long must it have taken? How long had Lift planned his retreat? How long, before the work began, did it take to visualize something of this proportion?

As he came to the door, he took his hand from the wall and crossed to the other side...and stopped. He froze for what seemed like a minute or two, not even aware if he was even thinking, but he went back to the door. He felt electrified and breathed heavily. Now was his chance. Everyone was asleep. Briefly, he felt a twinge as if he had started to get Livingston, but changed his mind. An argument would ensue, and the professor didn't want to leave empty-handed. At that moment, Wylie didn't care. He took a deep breath and turned the knob...and nearly collapsed. It was locked.

~*~

After an already sleepless night, Wylie now found himself on a jogging track, contemplating. It was still early in the morning, but he could not go to sleep. The rhythmic motion of his legs and his regular breathing calmed him enough to release him from panic and clear his mind. His thoughts had become jumbled, and he tried to sort them out, trying not to jump to conclusions. Every lesson he'd ever learned in his life had come to that, and that was why he was a reporter. He could not publish what he could not back up. There could be any number of reasons why the door had been locked. Perhaps Lift was paranoid, also, and just felt safer that way. Perhaps it was just a quirk, and the door wouldn't stay closed if it wasn't locked. Perhaps it was just a habit, and Lift hadn't given it a second thought. Perhaps, perhaps, perhaps. The only thing he knew was that a locked door really told him nothing.

There was a way to find out, but that posed other questions. Should he risk upsetting Lift by asking? Was there some rule of etiquette that would help him now? He thought, probably so. It would be odd to explain why he had tried to open the door in the first place. "Yes, Mr. Lift, I was going to run for my life, and I was hoping you could give me the key to the door." There was another thing. Why did it seem like an attempted escape to him? Escape from what? *I'm being too hard on the old man*, he thought. *It's a fault with* me. Then, he wondered why he was being so paranoid. But he was a reporter. Surely, after all he'd seen in his life, this assignment was not dangerous or even threatening at all, and he shouldn't be worrying.

The fact remained, however, that he was. He tried to relax, but the attempts were unsuccessful. What made this trip different than the others? Maybe it would tell him what his one true fear was. Psychology...that might best be answered by the professor, who might or might not help him. No, no. Now was not the time to let the doctor discover his weaknesses and perhaps later use them against him. He'd have to be alone on this one. So...why?

He slowed his pace, trying to cool down. As he continued to ponder the door, he felt guilty for thinking he shouldn't tell Livingston. After all, he really did not know what his reaction would be, and he shouldn't assume anything. Perhaps he'd have an early private conversation,

and Livingston could put some logic to
his ramblings, and he'd feel much better.
He didn't think Lift was yet awake.
Livingston might be.

# CHAPTER 5

It didn't take long for Livingston to answer the door, and Wylie thought he must have been anxious for company. He sat on the edge of the bed while the professor walked over to the desk and sat in the chair. Wylie tried to think of a way to begin. It seemed forever as he sat there in silence, but the professor was being unusually patient.

"Okay, this might be stupid," he started, hoping that if Lift were asleep, the microphones would be off and that he didn't record these conversations for later if the mics existed at all. "I was just out wandering and exploring the house. There's no reason for this, but I tried to open the door, and it was locked." It sounded trivial even as he spoke.

"What?" Livingston seemed confused. "Why did you try the door?"

"Like I said, there's probably no reason. I really don't know. Something just pulled me to it."

"I really don't think that was necessary."

Wylie realized that the professor thought it was insulting to Lift to try to leave in the middle of the night. "Look, I don't know why I tried the door. I don't know what I would have done if it had opened, either. I just...." He didn't know what he really hoped to gain from talking to Livingston and now began to regret his decision.

"It didn't open?"

He guessed that it had just sunk

in that the door had been locked. "No, it was locked. That was what bothered me. I know there are several possible explanations, and I don't know why this is so disturbing. I know it shouldn't be. I just don't want to jump to conclusions, and I can't sleep."

The professor wasn't listening and appeared to be concentrating. "Why would he have locked the door? There aren't people out here. Surely after twenty years, he would realize this is unnecessary. Why would he even *need* a lock on the door, for that matter?"

"Well, I thought maybe it was habit or something like that. Maybe he just feels better that way, after all of those years in the city."

The professor still pondered. "Perhaps, perhaps. You are right. There are too many possibilities, and we shouldn't blow this out-of-proportion."

"Yes, yes. I know. I really don't know why it bothers me. It's not as if Mr. Lift doesn't have other quirks, and I suppose they're all completely understandable. No one watching. He could do whatever he wanted, *however* he wanted. I mean, what would you do if you were alone for twenty years?"

"Go mad."

~*~

The knock sounded like thunder in the silence of his room and seemed to come in the middle of the night. He had lost all sense of time and felt completely disoriented. It took him a while to get out of bed, and he wasn't quite sure if he'd actually made it to sleep or not. He could barely walk in a straight line in his fatigue but managed to get to the door without significant injury. He cracked the door, expecting Livingston, but it was Wynne Lift, bright and energetic.

"Breakfast is being served if you would like to join me." He had a wide smile that made his eyes twinkle in their typical way.

"Yes, thank you." He tried to smile and not appear too groggy but was unsuccessful.

"Did you sleep all right?" Lift asked, his concern obvious and genuine.

Wylie couldn't think of a lie quickly but decided the truth was best anyway... well, maybe a half-truth. "No, not really. I think the absence of a day and night for me is throwing my circadian rhythms off."

"Oh, yes. That does take some adjustment. You should get used to it soon."

*How long are we going to be here?* Wylie wondered, then shook it off. "Yes, I hope so."

"If you'd like, you could have

another hour or two, and we'll make it a brunch."

"That's very nice of you, but I'll be okay. I'll see you there in a few minutes."

Lift acknowledged and walked away with a slight spring in his step. Wylie assumed Livingston had already been awakened but wanted to check on him personally. He dressed as quickly as he could and tried to slip down the hall without being seen. The phantom microphones surely caught him, but he hoped no one was watching.

Livingston answered his door with a puzzled expression on his face until he saw that it was Wylie in front of him and not Lift. "Is everything all right?"

Wylie pushed himself inside the room and closed the door. "I just wanted to make sure you wouldn't mention the door thing until we've had a chance to really discuss it between you and me. I feel like we're being paranoid here, and I don't want to offend Lift by asking him about it."

"Of course. I hadn't intended to, but we should talk later."

"I'm sorry, by the way."

"For what?"

"For the eating habits comment. I guess I had a little too much bravado and wanted to show off or something. It came out differently than I intended, and I took some of my frustrations out on you. I'm sorry about it all."

Livingston listened and seemed genuinely relieved and perplexed at the same time. "I think you and I have started out at odds, and some of it was me. I can't say it was all you. I wanted to control the assignment, as I've been working on this for some time, and I didn't want anyone else taking it away. Let's just attribute it to fatigue and move on."

Wylie nodded in agreement and smiled. "Good idea. I also think we should ask a few questions and see about getting even a partial interview today. Lift said something like we'd be adjusted to the time soon, but I'm really not anxious to stay long enough to get adjusted."

"How soon is 'soon'?"

Wylie shrugged. "Want to find out?"

A definite "No." Livingston shook his head with enthusiasm.

# CHAPTER 6

Lift was bubbly all through breakfast. Wylie didn't want to interrupt, but he felt like he was receiving a university lecture. Lift bragged about his creation and all the time put into it without specifying how much time that might have been. He gave them overviews of all the facilities without getting into the science of how they were done, like the still nagging fuel question that Wylie wanted to ask but couldn't think of how to bring up without sounding rude. He talked about human history and all the errors of the human race without saying whether this had anything to do with this major decision. Otherwise, the atmosphere was relatively casual, and the breakfast was very simple, just fruit after the heavy dinner the night before.

At last, Lift seemed to be winding down, and then he took a deep breath and smiled broadly. "Well, I'm sure I've talked your ears off! How about you? How are you doing this morning?"

Wylie, for once, waited for the professor to answer. Livingston smiled awkwardly, then admitted, "Well, I just wish I was sleeping better. Probably the circadian rhythms and all that. Just not adjusted to the lack of light. Perhaps we could go out for a while later on. It might help me adjust."

"Oh, we'll have time for plenty of that, don't you worry. Don't you worry. I feel like I'm just getting to know you fellows. I'd love to hear more about the outside world. What's been going on that I should know about?"

Livingston waited to be interrupted, but Wylie remained silent. Livingston wondered if he was brooding or thinking about last night. "Well, I suppose I could tell you what I'd learned about your family." He cleared his throat briefly and then took a deep breath. How to begin? He feared how Lift would take this news but knew that the man was chiefly interested in this particular topic, and they had yet to discuss it. "Your wife first. She never remarried. She lived in London for another five years to make sure you weren't coming back. Then she moved out to the country, nearer to her brother and his wife and children. Sadly, she committed suicide another five years later. No one knows why. She never left a note or discussed your leaving. Everyone assumes it was loneliness, but we'll never know for sure. Your daughter lives in New York, like Mr. Wylie. She has yet to marry, however. But she's working as a psychologist. Went to Harvard, as I understand it. She's very bright, but they say she has few friends. She seems the introspective type. I have yet to meet her, but I'd like to if you'd allow it."

"Oh, I can't stop what she'll do or not do. She's her own person, obviously. I'd have preferred she stay with me, of course, but I suppose it was unrealistic to think she might not want her own family or career."

"I would assume it was a difficult decision for her. If I speak to her, I can try to get word to you of what she said," Livingston proposed.

"Let's not worry about that for now, shall we? We still have so much to discuss. What of politics? What of the world at large? Any major events I should be aware of?"

"I'm not sure any of it is relevant to your life right now."

Lift's face colored, and his eyes darkened. "Who are you to decide what is relevant to me and what isn't?" he shouted. "I think I'll make that determination for myself if you don't mind!"

Both Livingston and Wylie were shocked into silence. Livingston stuttered after a while, then tried to regain his composure. "I'm sorry. I meant no offense. I just thought it might be disturbing to hear of the world's disasters when you're so far away from them."

"Oh. Well...quite right. Quite right. I imagine it might be a shock, but I can't say I'd like the truth to be hidden from me. Just the major events. Perhaps just the New York news, since it isn't as sentimental to me as London might be."

Wylie took a breath, nervous to speak after Lift's outburst. He explained the terrorist attacks in more detail, especially the 9/11 attacks. Lift's face registered genuine horror at the thought of so many lives lost. Wylie mentioned the election of the nation's first African-American president, as well as other events he thought might be interesting in any way. However, he was uncomfortable discussing things that were obviously personal, such as his reactions or feelings regarding the events that took place.

"At least there was some progress despite the setbacks," he concluded.

"That's good to hear, although I'm very sorry to hear about your people being killed. Horrible. Just horrible."

"We watched it on TV, even in the U.K. Everyone was following it, including the election later," Livingston added.

"Perhaps I don't want to hear the London news, after all. I don't think I could take it if something happened like that to my city." Wylie noted the use of the words "my city" by Lift.

"I'll keep it from you if you like. If you change your mind, I can always tell you later."

Lift brightened. "Oh, of course, of course. Fantastic."

Livingston shifted in his seat. "There is a subject I'd like to discuss with you if it's all right?" He waited and got a nod in response. "The interview. I know you may not have decided just yet, but I am curious if you've considered it."

"Yes, of course, I've considered it. But I still haven't decided. I suppose you could still write the story or article based on what I've already said, but I don't want to do a formal interview just yet. I'm not sure how I feel about baring my soul, as it were." He gave a disarming smile.

Livingston couldn't help but smile in response.

~*~

Another day, Lift showed them the library. It was as large as any large library in a large city, with thousands of books and other forms of literature. The professor and reporter started to wonder just how large this place really was. It must have been an enormous effort to construct it and the rest of the house, more than they had previously imagined. It must have taken years simply to collect all of the books. The library was built on several levels, with arches and columns around a large open space, with a reading room below on the bottom floor. A desk existed all on its own in a quiet corner, obviously there for writing and other such occupations. The other tables were of the coffee table type, with a few end tables sprinkled around with lamps resting on them. Like the other rooms, this one was lavishly furnished, although less formal than the rest of the — what? House? Cave?

Wylie immediately wondered how many of the volumes Lift had gone through by now. Surely the man must read a lot, being alone the last couple of decades. Perhaps Livingston wanted the article done now because it was a nice round number of years since Lift moved here. Perhaps it was simply the mysterious violin stories.

Livingston immediately began scanning the spines, looking for something to occupy his sleepless nights. Wylie had brought novels along with him in his baggage in an e-reader. Livingston had brought a couple of reports and a laptop but few books. There was no

Internet, so he'd simply been writing up notes. He assumed Wylie had been doing the same.

Lift happily bragged about his collection and what it contained. He particularly focused on science, art, and history in his non-fiction sections. He'd brought many different genres of fiction, knowing he'd want to change them as he got older, and he didn't want to tire of any one of them. He asked about current fiction and about what types of books the two others normally read. He wanted to know about their favorite books and what they were about. It was very obvious he was passionate about literature and could talk for hours on the subject.

Today Lift was all smiles, as usual. He listened with obvious interest about the plots and subplots of the various books both Wylie and Livingston discussed. He was a brilliant conversationalist, and again they wondered why he'd left England to come here. The time flew by, and Wylie and Livingston almost forgot any of their previous discomforts.

At last, Lift sighed deeply, grinning like a little child, then abruptly became the adult and assumed his host role. "Well, gentlemen, I suppose I'd better get started on a late lunch for all of us. I've neglected you both in the past couple of days, knowing you would be exhausted. I hope you don't think the worst of me!"

"No, sir. You've been more than gracious. I've enjoyed the time to think and relax a little." Livingston smiled, hoping Lift couldn't guess how anxious he'd been since he and Wylie had arrived.

"Excellent!" Lift responded with obvious delight, completely oblivious to the other two men's discomfort. They were both relieved by that.

Lift stood, thanked them both for

their conversation, then proceeded to the kitchen — or wherever he prepared their meals. Livingston then relaxed a little, still smiling slightly after their discussion. "He's really an excellent cook. I had no idea he had an interest in it at all. I suppose he *had* to develop an interest in it after moving here, though. I assume he had a personal chef in England, considering his busy lifestyle there."

Wylie pondered a moment. "Do you think his wife taught him, or his daughter?"

"Hmm. Don't know. Perhaps we can ask him. I don't suppose that's too personal a subject, don't you think?"

"No, I'm sure that's safe."

Livingston sighed, then stood. "Perhaps I'll pick up a novel or two to pass the time."

Wylie decided he might as well browse as well, despite the fact that he still had many books he hadn't yet read. The two men went off to explore in the time they had. After a time, Lift returned, saying that lunch was ready and apologizing for taking so long. Wylie frowned a little, thinking. He was still hidden by a large bookshelf, so he knew Lift hadn't seen the expression. However, the expression was only because he hadn't realized he'd been looking that long. He knew it might be misconstrued. He made his way downstairs, meeting Livingston on his way down the corridor and seeing, from the man's similar expression, that he'd been thinking the same thing.

"Time flies," he said under his breath to Livingston.

Livingston only grinned a little in response, following Lift and unwilling to be overheard.

# CHAPTER 7

As much as Wylie enjoyed the meals he'd had with Lift, he couldn't wait to be back in New York with a simple steak and baked potato. So far, everything had been vegan or a certain type of vegan. Without sunshine, there were certain foods that couldn't be grown, and Lift didn't have the resources to feed livestock. His facilities accommodated a lot more than Wylie had imagined and produced plenty of food for all three men. Apparently, this part of the plan had been in place before Lift knew his family wouldn't be joining him. However, there was not as much of a variety of foods that Wylie was used to. He missed his friends and family back home. He missed the theaters, museums, restaurants, and even the traffic sounds he was used to. He even missed seeing the water, something he'd hardly noticed when he was at home. Lift obviously had a water source of some kind tapped, but it wasn't the same as seeing the river or the sea, even if he never stepped in it. Here, he'd never have his toes in beach sand. Back home, he'd had to make a special trip to the beach, but he still managed a few times a year. He didn't think he could live somewhere without seeing water like that. He was already missing it, and it had only been a few days. Perhaps it was just not knowing when he'd see it again that made it seem so distant. Like it or not, he'd have to press the interview question some more, something he wasn't comfortable with. He had never been the high-pressure type and didn't want to become it, either. But at this point, he wanted to know whether he had a chance at all or if it would be better to cut his losses and head home.

Wylie tried to bring his attention back to the book he'd been reading, having chosen a volume from Lift's library, but didn't want to become too involved in it. For reasons he couldn't explain, he wanted to be able to put it down at a moment's notice and be able to walk away. However, he knew he'd be there long enough to read a little of it and possibly even to finish it. It was just the idea that he was going to be there long enough to finish it that was disturbing to him, as he didn't want to become involved in anything at all.

He'd taken some notes on his laptop, even though the outlets in the room were designed for British appliances. A previous trip to England meant he had a couple of adapters in his luggage. Otherwise, he wouldn't have even had that to keep him occupied and would be relying way too much on Lift. Eventually, the question of laundry would have to be brought up since he'd only brought a couple of changes of clothing to save space. Wylie thought of the long journey to get back home and missed his dog, waiting for him back in his apartment, although he knew Lauren would be taking good care of him. She'd done this for him plenty of times before. Wylie knew he owed her a lot for everything. She and her husband were good friends of his now and no longer just his landlords. However, he knew he'd have to make other arrangements soon. The old couple didn't have the energy to keep up with the walks as much anymore, especially Lauren's husband.

Sighing, he tried again to focus on the book. At home, he always liked to have paper books. It was a small comfort, then, to have one in his hands instead of the e-reader he usually traveled with. It felt good simply to have to turn real pages, to see the light pass through the paper as he lifted it. Still, he couldn't get into the story. He felt very distracted. Abruptly, he closed it and stood. He might as well do a little more exploring or go back to the jogging track, anything to clear his head and help him sleep.

He wandered the corridors in the semi-darkness, remembering what some rooms were for and not others. The ones he didn't know, he'd enter briefly and try to create a mental map of the whole place. He could only estimate the dimensions, but the place was simply too immense to keep track of it all. He'd been mapping small parts a bit at a time. Tonight, he wandered until he arrived back at the library.

Before he'd even reached the doorway, however, he heard music. He inched forward, curious but not wanting to be seen himself. Dim light emanated from the room, but he couldn't make out any shadows that might tell him whom the occupant was or where he was situated. Slowly he crept along the wall, peering cautiously around the doorframe but remaining in shadow.

Lift was seated on one of the sofas, listening to a stereo system that was playing classical music. Wylie came a little closer, scarcely daring to breathe. Lift was sifting through papers of some sort and humming quietly. Wylie stood on tiptoe to see over the man's shoulder without moving any closer and saw that it was all sheet music. The violin was nowhere to be seen, but Lift was sorting through all of it and laying some of them aside for future use. Wylie backed off slowly, trying not to make a sound. The music was not very loud and would not provide much cover. He made his way slowly back down the corridor until he was alone in another part of the house, then found his way back to the bedroom he'd been using. He'd learned an important lesson, however. Apparently, he and Livingston weren't the only ones up at night.

~*~

Morning found Livingston in Wylie's bedroom again, looking as if he'd neglected to shave, despite the en-suites for each room.

"Are you all right?" asked Wylie, concerned.

"Yes, yes, yes. I'm fine," came the reply, a little impatiently. "I've just been thinking. I know I'm not sleeping well, and I'm assuming you aren't either. I believe I slept better out in the open than I'm doing here. What if we just camp outside tonight? Perhaps it would reset my clock to the right time. I feel like I'm in a casino or something."

Wylie laughed despite himself. "I hope it can't hurt to ask. I'm getting cabin fever in here so many nights. I hardly know what to do to relax. Maybe both of us just need to see the sky."

At breakfast, Livingston was anxious and afraid to spoil the pleasant mood by broaching the subject. However, his desire to be outside was stronger than his fear of being shouted at. Eventually, he asked simply, "Would it be all right to go out for a bit later on? We can watch the sunset or something. I know I'd like to watch the stars come out."

Lift seemed a little perplexed and

simply stared at him. When Livingston didn't get an answer, he began to wonder if Lift had understood him or even heard him. He was about to repeat himself when Lift regained his color and stammered, "W…w…well, of course we can. I don't see why not." He smiled then, and it seemed genuine, but Livingston was disconcerted. *Can we, now?*

Wylie said, "Well, we appreciate that. Just a little change of scenery might do wonders."

Lift had a strange expression on his face just then, and Wylie's smile died. Before he had a chance to do or say anything, Livingston stood, stretching.

"Great breakfast. Thank you so much. I believe I'll have a try at the jogging track today." He was newly invigorated by the idea of going outside, and he didn't know what to do with his energy.

Lift recovered his expression. "If you don't mind, gentlemen, I'd like to have a small performance tonight in the library. I do love to play the violin, but it's been years since I've performed for an audience. Would you mind?"

"No, sir. We don't mind. We could just as well do it out of doors, however." Livingston's smile was still there, but the invigorated feeling was gone.

"Well, the acoustics are much better in the library. There will be plenty of time for sunsets, Mr. Livingston. Pardon, *Dr.* Livingston." He smiled broadly, recalling the famous explorer by the same name. "Perfect."

Livingston looked at Wylie, who was trying not to feel deflated and disappointed. Worry was transferred between them telepathically.

# CHAPTER 8

Left to themselves, the researcher and the reporter both decided to go to the jogging track after all. "We tried. What do we do now?" Wylie asked as he rounded a corner. He had to slow down a bit to allow the older man to keep up.

Livingston was already breathing heavily and did not speak for a moment. He did not slow down, however, and kept up his pace even as he pondered the question. "Well, he did say he goes out himself. How often do you think he does so?"

"Not often enough, I'd say."

Livingston thought again. "Well, surely the man gets tired of being in a place with recirculated air. He's got to go out sometimes. I haven't seen him go out personally, but I'll admit that I haven't spent much time in view of the door."

Wylie sighed as much as his breathing allowed. "I'll admit that I haven't either. I've been more interested in trying to figure out how this was done. He had to have had a team of people working on this, possibly even a very large workforce. What happened to them? Surely we can talk to them and get what Lift hasn't explained. At least one person would want to talk to us, I'd think."

"Hmm."

He didn't have to say what they were both thinking. *If we get out of here.*

Definitively, Wylie declared, "We're going to have to ask about the interview, you know? Yes or no, and that's it. We can't stay here forever. I've got loads of other things to do, and I'm sure you have to get back to your classes. He can't keep us here if we want to go, right? That's just our paranoia. It's just this house, or whatever you want to call it."

Livingston seemed doubtful. "Perhaps."

"Either way, we need to either get what we came for or leave with nothing. I don't want to wait until he makes up his mind on his own. Do you?"

"No. Absolutely not. You're right. I've got too many other projects to dally on only this one. I'll admit this would be better if Lift did the interview, but there are many other people we could speak with to get this story. We'll have to ask how this was all done. He seems proud of his achievement. I'd bet he wants to talk about it."

"Perhaps."

Both were silent except for a moment, except for their breathing. They turned another corner in thought, then continued on the straightaway. "Have you tried the door again?" Livingston wondered.

Wylie couldn't tell if it was a criticism or a genuine inquiry. "No. Why?"

"Maybe he's been out, and we didn't see him. Maybe he unlocked it or forgot to lock it. We could check."

Wylie hated to bring it up but felt he had to. "Look, I was up one night, wandering and looking around. Lift was up, too. I don't know if he sleeps well at night either. We really need to find a way to do it without him seeing us. I don't want to have to answer his questions, you know? Besides, with our baggage, I don't think we could slip out unnoticed."

Livingston let out a ragged breath. "There has to be a way. There has to be. We've asked politely. Perhaps we should be less polite."

~*~

Lift's playing was beautiful. Despite any other feelings, they were genuinely impressed. Lift obviously had had a lot of time to practice and improve. One of the few things that anyone knew about Lift was that he was a great violinist, although somewhat reclusive. But the two men in the audience had no idea that he was as brilliant as he was. He could have been famous, such was his talent. Although they had wanted to go outdoors, Lift had been correct about the acoustics in the library. They applauded politely between selections, and Lift glowed in their praise.

Eventually, however, they were all

exhausted and Lift put away his violin and set aside the music to be filed away the next day. Wylie decided to ask again, "May we go outside for a while?"

"It's a bit late for that, isn't it? I'm off to bed."

"Well, you don't have to come with us. We thought we'd spend a night under the stars, camping. I think it would do us some good to see the sky again."

Lift's good mood was gone. "Well, I don't know why you'd want to do that. The beds I've provided are more than comfortable."

"No, it's not that. They are. Of course, they are. It's just that we haven't seen the sky in a long time—"

"It can wait for another time, Mr. Wylie. Right now, I just want to go to bed. I'll see you in the morning."

Exasperated, he stopped Lift with his arm. "Please. I don't think it's a lot to ask. We're not leaving, just spending the night outside. You know I want to interview you, so I won't leave just yet. But I think it's only a small thing, and surely you can see, since you yourself go out sometimes, why we'd want to do such a thing."

"Remove your hand, Mr. Wylie, and go to bed. We can discuss this at another time." His expression was murderous.

Wylie backed down, still exasperated, and looked over to Livingston, who looked horrified. "Please, Mr. Lift. We'll be back for breakfast. We've been polite, but you really can't keep us here indefinitely."

"Who said I was keeping you here? That's a strange way of saying 'thank you for your hospitality' to someone who took you in when you came here unannounced. I think I've gone out of my way to make you both comfortable. If you want further favors, then perhaps you should let me get to know you better. That will have to wait. I'm going to bed. Good night."

And, then, he was gone, turning the lights out behind him without waiting for the others to depart.

# CHAPTER 9

They met in Livingston's room after they were sure Lift was gone. They had no idea where his room was to be completely sure he was asleep, but they knew he was no longer in that part of the house. "We have to ask again in the morning. He can't have the excuse of being tired then. We can ask about the interview and get a definite answer, or else leave it and go home. Let him know we want to leave for good. He has to see reason eventually," Wylie suggested.

"How do we know he can be reasonable? It's been twenty years, and he hasn't had to be reasonable. He hasn't had to compromise or deal with others' feelings. Here, he always gets his own way." Livingston was gritting his teeth in his frustration.

"He seems rational. A little odd, but somewhat rational, I think. We should be able to convince him. Either that, or we need to find his room and the key to the door."

"Sneak out? I want to go home, but I also want to do it the right way. I think you were right when you said we have to convince him. I don't know how, but there has to be some way or other. Maybe we can just be unpleasant, and he'll *ask* us to leave, eh?"

Wylie sighed. "Do you really want to wait until he gets that annoyed? Besides, I'm sure we haven't really seen his real angry side. Do you want to see it?"

Livingston sighed now. "No, not really. Well, what do you think we should do? The key could be anywhere."

Wylie thought a moment. "Well," he said, "there are two of us. We should be able to get out that door, key or no key."

"It's built into the rock, Mr. Wylie. The jamb is made of rock. We can't just bust it down."

"Well, what do you suggest then, Livingston? I'm open," Wylie growled.

"I don't know. I really don't know. Perhaps we should spend a little more time going around the house in a more directed manner. Instead of just trying to pass time and learn more about the man, why don't we look for something to work the door with? There has to be something here. This place is enormous, and I know we haven't seen it all. We've been going through it without prying too deeply, being that we are only guests. We can be a little more thorough now."

Wylie calmed slightly. "Sure. I don't know how to pick a lock, but perhaps we can figure it out. Or were you thinking along the lines of a crowbar or something?"

"Oh, the crowbar, Mr. Wylie. The crowbar. Definitely."

~*~

Wylie was still too anxious to sleep, despite his conversation with Livingston. He didn't want to wait until the old man was awake. Instead of trying to read or going to the jogging track as before, he went from room to room looking for metal pieces sturdy enough to chip away at the rock or perhaps through the door. He hadn't paid attention to what the door might have been made of when they first entered the house, but it felt heavy, and he was certain it would be difficult, even if they had an axe, to cut through it. The rock wasn't granite. It had to be soft enough to work quickly, given the scale of the place they had carved out of it. With the right tools, it had to be possible to work the stone, or the place could never have been.

He didn't think there was any point in searching the other bedrooms. They were all very similar to each other, and he'd searched his own and Livingston's before Livingston decided to go to bed. He'd thought of the bed frames themselves, but they were of very sturdy wood and would have needed a tool of the type they were looking for just to take them apart. He'd been hoping for the cheap metal kind he had at home. The lamps were somewhat fragile and wouldn't take much pressure to break. The rest of the furniture was very heavy and too impractical to drag out to the door.

He decided that perhaps his best chance of finding metal tools might be in the kitchen, which he'd never seen, but he assumed it could not be far from the dining room. Quietly he made his way there, then went into an adjoining room, thinking to start there. It wasn't the kitchen, but he dutifully searched through every cabinet. It was obviously storage, but not where the utensils were. It was basically a large china cabinet, with various sets of casual and formal dinnerware stored in a display of sorts. There were more plates in each set than would be required by Lift's own family. There were more bedrooms than would have been required as well, he reflected. Had Lift intended his staff to move there? Had he even asked them before he'd begun building?

Putting the puzzle aside, he moved

on. There was a short corridor that also branched off the dining room, and he went down that next. It ended in what was obviously a kitchen but a large restaurant-style kitchen. Immediately he opened the cabinets nearest the stove, thinking the pans would be close by. He found a few cast-iron pans that would be heavy enough but would not work to actually chisel the rock. They might work as a hammer, however. So he continued searching, hoping to find a makeshift chisel.

Suddenly there was a shuffling at the doorway, and Wylie spun around to see Lift standing there. "What are you doing, going through my things?" he demanded.

Wylie stammered, "W...w...well, I...I just.... I just got a little hungry, that's all. I was going to make a snack."

Lift smiled then. "Oh, don't trouble

yourself. I'll make you something. Go back to your room, and I'll bring it out to you."

"I don't want to trouble you, sir. I don't mind. I actually like to cook at home, so I have no problem — "

"No, no, it's no trouble. I wouldn't be a very good host if I made you do your own cooking, now would I?"

"Really, I don't mind," Wylie tried to insist.

"Nonsense. Go on to your room. I'll just prepare something simple, so don't worry about me feeling troubled."

Unsure, Wylie put away the pan he'd had in his hand. He decided to feign gratefulness and explore more later that night — or if it must be, the next night. "Thank you so much, sir. I appreciate it." Then, he did as he was told and went back to his room, still trying to come up with a plan that did not involve violence against the old man.

# CHAPTER 10

After dealing with the meal he hadn't really wanted and speaking for a short time with Mr. Lift, Wylie was too tired to continue exploring. He fell asleep not long after but slept restlessly and had disturbing dreams. Sometimes he was running through dark corridors, pursued by unseen foes. Sometimes he was in crowded rooms with light fixtures that were hardly working, and he had a sensation of being watched. They always ended with a feeling like he was falling from a great height, and he'd awake in a cold sweat.

The knock was not completely unexpected this time, but he felt ill-prepared to deal with it in his present state. He tossed a little, trying to get up but unable to get his limbs working properly for a moment. He groaned, finally able to sit up. The knock was more insistent this time. "Coming," he called, not sure whether he could be heard or not. He shuffled his way to the door, stubbing his toe on the desk chair on his way. Hopping for a few steps and trying not to curse, he opened the door with a grimace, which was not how he wanted to greet his visitor.

It was Livingston, looking uneasy and anxious to get out of the hallway. Wylie stepped aside to allow him to enter, then closed the door, still not very alert but trying to wake up fully.

"What's the matter?"

Livingston smiled a little

sheepishly. "Well, I haven't been sleeping. I'm still feeling quite closed-in." He paused a moment, thinking. "I did do a little exploring last night, but I heard Lift at your door, and I had to wait until he'd gone to continue."

"He caught me in the kitchen. I had to pretend I was hungry, so he made me a snack. I didn't want to seem ungrateful, so I chatted with him for a few minutes."

"Well, I wasn't really going to talk about that. Anyway, I hid for a few moments, then decided to check the door. I'm afraid it's still locked. I'm at a loss, really."

Wylie had expected this, so he wasn't as disturbed as he'd expected to be. "He has to have tools. He has a lot of equipment here that has to be maintained. It's been twenty years. It has to have broken down at some point. He's got to have screwdrivers and hammers, you'd think."

"Oh, I agree. I was also wondering how he kept this place up. Some rooms are fairly dusty, but everything looks fairly well-kept. Is that all he does all day, just taking care of the house?"

Wylie had wondered the same thing but really hadn't thought much about it recently. "It's not impossible. I just wonder how so many people have kept quiet about all of this. There's also a large amount of space that's not being used, I noticed. I wondered if he'd meant his staff to join him, along with his family."

Livingston thought this sounded plausible and said so. "So, he's somewhat reclusive, but not completely solitary. I wonder why he went through with it in the end. He knew he'd be alone. It can't just have been the expense. He had enough money to do it twenty times over.

I just find it hard to believe he'd choose to be alone."

Wylie just said, "I really don't know. I wish he'd tell us."

Livingston sighed. "I don't know if we'll ever find out. I can ask about the interview again, but I'm starting to wonder if he ever intended to go through with it at all."

"I'm not sure."

Sighing again, Livingston suggested, "Why don't we try the equipment rooms next? The generator room, perhaps, or something of that sort?"

Wylie didn't have any other ideas, so he nodded. He was still tired and trying to ignore his throbbing foot.

Another knock sounded at the door. There was no doubt about who it could be. Wylie limped to the door and answered it, forcing a smile. "How are you this morning?" he asked.

Lift was not smiling and looked a little concerned but in an annoyed sort of way. "Have you seen your friend? He's not in his room."

Wylie looked back at the professor, then back at Lift. "Well, he's here in my room. We were discussing our plans for the day. Would you like to join us?" Might as well pretend nothing suspicious was going on.

"Oh, thank you, Mr. Wylie. Perhaps another time. I was just coming to let you know that breakfast will be a little late this morning. I slept a little later than I'd meant to. You're welcome to leftovers from last night."

"Oh, no. We'll be fine. Thank you. I can wait. We'll be with you whenever you're ready."

Lift left a little reluctantly, it seemed, a look of mistrust on his face as he turned away.

~*~

Livingston was obviously uncomfortable. Wylie knew his claustrophobia hadn't gotten any better, but Livingston was very determined and was facing it with a great deal of bravery. He couldn't hide his occasional glances at the ceiling or the walls, but the fear was not evident on his face. He still hadn't shaved, and his already wild grey curls were even wilder since they'd arrived. Wylie could picture him tearing his hair out at night in his distress. Despite this, Livingston had asked again about getting an interview, even if it was only a partial one.

Lift looked a little as if Livingston had asked about his sexual habits or something equally as private. "If that's all you're interested in, I'm a bit disappointed. I'd hoped we could spend some time getting to know each other before I answered that question."

Livingston took a deep breath, trying to remain calm. "I'm sorry, sir, but that is the main reason we came. I suppose we just want to know whether it will happen at some point, or if we're better off looking for this story elsewhere or giving up on the story altogether."

"Well, I don't think you need to rush things. I think things are moving along nicely, and I don't see any reason to change something that's already going very well."

Livingston swallowed his fear again. "They may be going nicely for you, but we've really got to be going. I have other obligations in the outside world. I can't leave them forever."

Lift didn't say a word for a while, but his complexion reddened in his anger, and his eyes went wide. "I'm very sorry to hear you aren't enjoying yourself, but I don't see how you expect me to decide on something that may give away my location or other such information in only a few days. I need more time. It's obvious you don't understand me, so you really should take more time to do so."

"What if we just spoke of the house and how it was built? Surely that's a safe subject. You don't have to give away anything personal. Just an overview of the technology required. If you can't do that, could you please refer us to the people actually responsible for executing the project? You can do that without giving away geological details that might identify the location," Livingston persisted.

"Any information you need is available in the library."

Livingston looked dismayed. "But it's a very large library!"

"Well, all the technology is in there if you take the time to look."

"That could take years, sir. I just don't have that kind of time."

Lift ground his teeth a little, trying not to lose his temper, but doing a poor job of it. "And you think I can give you all of that information off the top of my head? You think I know about engineering and can give you formulas and diagrams? Or, do you think I know every volume that's in there, where it's located, and what information is in each one?"

"Okay, just one question. We'll start there. Where does the water come from?" There. How hard can this be?

"There's an aquifer below us. Can I tell you how we engineered everything around it, though? No."

"What about power? You have a lot of generators, but I don't see any fuel stored."

"The water, Mr. Livingston."

Livingston ignored the slight. "Yes, but *how*?"

"Look in the library. It's all there. You expect me to do all the work researching for you?"

"Well, no, sir. But I'm not an engineer. It would all be above my head. What if we could speak with the people who built this place? Such a unique place. Surely some of them would remember it."

"I'm really not comfortable with that now. I don't know what they'd say about me or the house."

"I'll edit anything out that gives it away."

"No, Mr. Livingston. Figure it out on your own." And with that, he rose, fuming, still red in the face, but now breathing heavily, and his hands balled into fists. He left the dishes and disappeared.

Wylie spoke for the first time. "Well, he's got to be getting annoyed by now."

# CHAPTER 11

Lift was so furious he didn't reappear for the usual lunch hour. Plates were left at their bedroom doors as a courtesy, but Lift did not, apparently, want to have the usual conversations along with the meal. This suited the two just fine. They ate quickly, both in Livingston's room this time, and planned a little more exploration for the afternoon. They agreed that if they ran into Lift, they would pretend to be doing something completely benign until such a time as they could go back to it unobserved. They hadn't been downstairs much and decided to start there since that was where the equipment rooms were most likely located. The stairs were still marble, as in the rest of the house, but were scored at the edges to prevent slipping. By now, some of this had worn down, but not so much that it was hazardous. This part of the house wasn't as frequently used.

They'd decided previously that they would split at this point in order for the search to go more quickly. Wylie headed for the generator room, or what he thought was the generator room, Livingston for the water heater and other plumbing fixtures. The generator room, on its own, was probably best explored by both men and not just one, as it was immense, but Wylie did his best to be thorough, wincing at every sound as he explored the equipment cabinets.

A tool chest became visible as Wylie neared the back of the room, skipping over the generators themselves since it was unlikely there would be tools left there. He tried not to get his hopes up, preparing himself for disappointment, but hope sprung up in him nonetheless. Drawer after drawer he opened, finding wrenches of varying sizes mostly, along with pliers and a rather large socket wrench set.

Disappointment started to rear its ugly head when suddenly he opened the last drawer and was rewarded with a large assortment of screwdrivers, and happily, a few hammers. He could hardly contain his joy but tried to think clearly and not act rashly. Would Lift find these items missing if he took them now? What would happen in that case? Still, he took one screwdriver that seemed sturdiest, although they all seemed to be top quality, with spares of each one. He sifted through the hammers carefully, testing a few of them on the tops of the screwdriver for size without actually striking anything. Finally, he decided on the best one and set out to find Livingston.

The professor was carrying a selection of pliers with a smile on his face, although Wylie couldn't think of what he meant to do with them. Wylie presented the tools he'd found in an almost formal manner, then broke out into a childish grin. The usually dour professor smiled back with obvious enthusiasm. Wylie couldn't help but voice his curiosity by asking, "What are the pliers for?" He was amused rather than criticizing.

Livingston didn't take offense and laughed a little. "Well, I thought we might work the doornails, but those might work better!"

Despite their obvious success, they decided to keep searching the house, knowing an escape attempt would have to be made in whatever they deduced to be nighttime. As they went along, finding nothing else of interest or usefulness, Livingston came to a locked door. At first, he didn't seem to recognize the significance of that and continued to go down the corridor. Realization hit him abruptly, and he rushed back, pulling Wylie with him.

"This door is locked!" he exclaimed.

Wylie seemed uninterested, then realized what Livingston was trying to say. Why would Lift lock a door *inside* his own house? Was this the time to find out? No, not yet.

"We'd need to muffle the sound," he said. "Let's get some towels from the bathrooms or something."

"What? Now?"

"Do you want to wait until tonight?" Wylie was still trying to think of whether this was something he preferred, as well.

"What do you think? I think we should wait. I don't know how long this will take, and Lift might find us. I'm sure there's a secret here he wouldn't want us discovering."

"Why would he lock this door? The only person here is himself. He can't be thinking to keep himself out of a room in his own house."

"I don't know. Perhaps your question will be answered tonight."

~*~

They went back to their rooms to while away the time and appear as normal and non-threatening as possible. Wylie's internal clock was so screwed up he realized he'd gotten up without shaving. He went and did so, then paced around, making up notes in his head and trying to organize his thoughts. He hadn't been to the jogging track in a couple of days. Perhaps he should do that, he pondered, just to help him relax.

Livingston took some notes and did some writing, trying to compose a paper that might never be completed. When this didn't go satisfactorily, he picked out one of the books he'd chosen from the library and tried to focus on it. He'd purposely chosen a mystery, a genre he read only occasionally at home. Most of the time, he spent his reading doing research, but since he'd come here, he felt like he wanted some sort of escape from his own ordinary life.

The knock reverberated through the room, causing Livingston to jump from his chair suddenly. He answered, expecting Wylie, but got Lift instead. The man was smiling from ear to ear, acting as if nothing had happened. "Yes?" Livingston asked nervously.

"Dinner will be ready shortly! I hope you're hungry." He was beaming.

"Of course. I'll be there in a few minutes. Thank you." He was perplexed but trying not to show it.

Lift nodded in response and walked away, humming a tune.

The knock was equally unexpected at Wylie's door, and a similar conversation ensued. Wylie wandered to Livingston's room afterward, a little unsure of himself, then knocked on Livingston's door.

"I'm coming," the professor said as he answered it, then saw who he was addressing. "Oh, sorry. How are you?"

"What just happened? I'm sure he invited you to dinner, too."

Livingston thought a moment but couldn't come up with an answer. "I have no idea. He's pretty unpredictable. Who knows?"

Both men made their way to the dining room, where the formal china was laid out, with silverware for several courses. They each exchanged glances, afraid to comment.

Lift entered, wearing somewhat formal attire, despite the fact that he was the only one available to serve the dishes. "Ah. There you are. I'll bring out the appetizers for you, gentlemen. Please be seated." He departed instantly.

The two sat, still not speaking. The meal was laid out, course by course, as if in a fine restaurant. The only incongruity was that Lift joined them at the table while they ate. He behaved in a somewhat different manner than before, but he seemed to be partly playing a role. He never mentioned the argument from earlier in the day, nor did he refer to any of the concerns that had been mentioned in that conversation. The other two men avoided the subject as well, preferring to keep everything limited to small talk, drawing Lift out into memories of his family before the split. They also avoided letting this get too personal. They shared their own memories, hoping Lift would sympathize with their desire to see their families again. He seemed oblivious, however, treating these stories as he did their discussion of literature, which seemed like ages ago. They didn't press the issue and let Lift determine the course of the conversation, keeping it light and pleasant. *Everyone* was doing a little playacting that evening.

Eventually, they'd grown exhausted, especially the professor and reporter, who were having the most trouble with their roles and trying desperately to keep Lift from noticing. Lift wished them goodnight, then began to clear the dishes. They excused themselves, saying they were going to the jogging track, which was actually true. They felt like burning off some of the calories they'd consumed, and they knew it was another way of killing time and helping them keep their minds on something else. They didn't know what to make of their strange dinner.

Both men went back to their rooms afterward to shower. However, neither could nap, having just exercised and also being apprehensive about their late-night snooping. Livingston was especially impatient, eventually so much so that he went off, searching the house, and finally satisfied himself that Wynne Lift had gone to bed. Anxiously he rushed Wylie out of his room and back downstairs to the locked door. He now noticed that the door was locked from the outside, where Lift could easily just use the key. Surely the man had one. A sense of foreboding came over him, and he almost talked himself out of trying to open the door. But no, he *had* to know. Wylie was already covering the screwdriver with a towel and angling it so it was under the doornail's head. He began striking it with the hammer, panicking that the sound was still terrifyingly loud without any carpeting to muffle the sound. Livingston went back upstairs to act as a lookout. The sound wasn't as loud up there due to the angle in the corridor that didn't allow sound to travel as easily in that direction.

Finally, Wylie came to get him. He had the door off the hinges and then began to work it from side to side, with help from the older man. Eventually, they managed to pull it free, and a black space yawned in front of them. Livingston swallowed his anxiety and felt along the wall for a light switch. Finding it, he turned on the light, then both men saw that there was another stairway leading downward. Livingston turned to look back once at Wylie, then took a deep breath and started down. When he reached the bottom, he froze, and Wylie tumbled into him.

"What is it?" Wylie asked before seeing the terrible story for himself.

The room itself was cavernous and lit by several crystal chandeliers. There were many long dining tables lined with fine linens, crystal, china, and what may have once been a meal. After all the years that had passed, there was no longer any odor, although each table was ringed by raggedly-dressed human skeletons.

Wylie was breathless for a moment, then asked, "Who are they?" He didn't necessarily expect a response.

He didn't get one for a long moment as Livingston began to look for details. He was afraid to approach any of the skeletons, but he noticed that their clothes, although partly disintegrated through time, were not the clothes of the wealthy or even of Lift's previous servants. There were so many skeletons around so many tables, each in coveralls, that he could hardly grasp the scope of it.

"They're the workers," he whispered.

"Why?" came Wylie's next question.

"You saw how private the man is and how desperate he was to conceal his location. He didn't want them talking!"

"How did they die? What about his servants? Where are *they*?"

Livingston thought briefly, then answered, "Poison. Gas. Don't know. Don't care."

Wylie pondered this a moment, then grabbed Livingston's arm. "We've got to get out of here *now*!"

# CHAPTER 12

They snatched up their tools and the towel at the top of the stairs as they fled, running without regard to safety on the marble tiles. Livingston slipped once and nearly fell, turning a corner toward the main stairway. They both scrambled up the stairs two or three at a time and turned to head toward the door. Too late, Wylie saw a shadow on the Queen Anne sofa that he had first noticed upon entering the house of Wynne Lift. He stopped, and Livingston slid into him from behind.

"And just where do you think

you're going?" came a voice from the shadows. It was obvious who was there. Wylie knew they were all alone, and the voice was only too familiar.

Wylie decided it was too late for etiquette. He'd seen what the man was capable of. "The game is up, Lift. We've seen your secret room downstairs."

"And what room would that be?" Lift stood from the sofa and came into the soft light of the sconce on the wall. He was holding a gun in his right hand, aimed right at Wylie and the professor.

Both Livingston and Wylie were edging toward the door, knowing they'd be stopped if they tried to escape, but angling toward their only goal. Livingston answered Lift's question. "The banquet room downstairs with your other guests in it!"

"What did they ever do to you, Lift?" continued Wylie. "Surely, they would have kept your secret. They didn't have to die, you know?"

"Oh, no, they didn't. But they didn't want to stay." Lift's voice was far away and almost child-like as he replied.

It was that moment that Livingston and Wylie both knew Lift had gone insane. He'd been irrational and unpredictable, but that could have been explained away before. They knew Lift would have no qualms about keeping them here, one way or another.

Wylie wanted to keep Lift distracted, to keep talking to him. "But they're gone now, Lift. They can't speak to you or keep you company. Surely you can see that you should have just let them go."

"No. I visit them. I keep the food and wine coming, and they are grateful for every moment. I could spend hours there, you know. They love it when I play the violin."

Wylie couldn't tell if Lift really meant what he was saying or was trying to appear more insane than he had already seemed. "No. No. They don't. They're gone. They're beyond caring if they have food or wine or entertainment."

"But, that's where you're wrong. They talk to me. They do. Surely you see that if you would just talk to them."

No, Lift really was that mad. Wylie now knew. Livingston slipped the screwdriver out of Wylie's hand behind his back and tried to move away, slowly making his way backward and behind Lift. *Keep talking, Wylie*, he thought.

"You don't hear the silence coming from that room?"

"Well," Lift said, "they're not as lively as the two of you. I really enjoy our conversations much, much more. You're both well-read and appreciate the arts. I feel like I can speak to you on my own level, you know? With them, it's almost as a teacher to a group of students."

Wylie became aware of another thing. Lift wasn't going to let them go. There was no pleading or rationalizing with him. He wanted them alive, but he'd take them dead.

"Why didn't you let them go? What was so important about keeping them here?"

"I...I just wanted company."

Wylie was confused. "You wanted to leave London to live in *this* kind of isolation, but you still wanted company?"

"Well, I...I thought I wouldn't be completely alone. I thought I would have opportunities for conversation when I wanted them. I thought my family would join me. When they didn't want to, I was willing to try on my own, but I got lonely. Surely you can understand that."

"But why didn't you ask them before you built this place? Why didn't you make sure you were going to *have* company?"

"Well, someone would want to stay, wouldn't they? Who wouldn't? It's a beautiful house, and I would take good care of them."

"Like the workers?"

Lift nodded enthusiastically. "Yes. Like the workers."

"How did you do it?" Wylie asked. "Poison? Gas?"

"Oh, no. I wouldn't do something like that." Lift actually seemed confused.

"The workers! How did you do it?" Wylie shouted.

He could see Livingston quietly inching away, no longer in sight of Lift but trying not to draw his attention. The urgency in his voice must have given something away because Lift turned and gestured with the gun for Livingston to go back to where Wylie was standing.

"Why do you assume I did anything? I just convinced them to stay, is all."

"No! No. That's not it. That's *not* it. I know you remember. You put something in the food, right?"

"I really don't know what you're talking about. You're becoming tiresome tonight. Just go back to bed, if that's where you really were, and we'll discuss this in the morning when I've had time to rest." He pointed toward the hallway with the expression of a father disciplining his naughty children.

The reporter and professor saw their chances of escape dwindling away. If they went back to bed, they'd never leave. Lift would find a way of keeping them there. He'd poison their breakfast or shoot them in their sleep.

Desperation crept into Livingston's voice, despite his intention to remain calm. "You can't keep us here! We have obligations and family out there! You are being very selfish! Surely you want us to be happy. You know we want to leave. Just let us leave!"

"No. Not tonight. Go back to bed. Everything will be better in the morning. It always is. You'll see. You'll be past these childish emotions. Now, if you don't go quietly, I will use the gun. I am a doctor of sorts. I had to keep myself healthy all of these years on my own. I can treat you, as well. I promise you'll recover. But it will be painful in the meantime."

Livingston was growing more desperate. "You can't do that! This life isn't for everyone. You did it to yourself, but that was your own choice. You can't expect everyone to want to do the same thing. Your wife and daughter didn't even come."

That was the wrong thing to say. Livingston heard the pop of the gun as if from a long distance. It seemed to take ages for the bullet to reach him. He leapt to the side just in time to avoid a serious leg wound, and then he tumbled to the floor, lying where he had fallen and praying there would be no more shots.

Wylie leapt toward the gun as the rebound kicked it upward. He held Lift's hands and the gun in both of his hands as they struggled, trying to gain control of their only weapon. Wylie was younger but not as tall or broad-chested as Lift. They kicked and fought, knowing it would be to the death. Wylie tried to throw punches but would end up loosening his grip on the gun. Wylie was not anxious to kill but was desperate to escape and didn't want to die there. He didn't know if the bullet had grazed

Livingston or had planted directly into his leg, but he knew the next shot would not be a warning shot. He knew the leg wound might as well have been a kill shot, as the desert would kill Livingston even if the bullet didn't. A wounded man stood little chance against the hazards of the return journey.

Lift knew this was it for him. He'd keep his prizes, or he'd be dead. He fought with a strength Wylie never knew he had. Lift should have been overpowered by now, Wylie thought, grunting with effort as he tried to wrest the gun from Lift's hands. Wylie's knee came up, aiming for Lift's groin, but he missed as Lift brought his own leg up to block and almost tripped Wylie as his leg came back down. Wylie lost precious inches, however, and the taller Lift began slowly turning the gun downward.

Suddenly, a hot expulsion of breath

came from Lift, and a look of shock came over his face. He went limp and crumpled on top of a confused Wylie, who was pinned beneath him. Wylie shoved Lift to one side and saw that blood dribbled from a head wound. The screwdriver was embedded in the base of Lift's scull, and Livingston looked devastated but triumphant at the same time.

"Are you all right?" he said, offering his hand to Wylie.

Wylie could hardly believe it was over. He reached out to take Livingston's hand. "Yeah. Yeah." But, he was thinking, *No, no. I'll never be all right.*

The professor bent to take the gun from Lift's hand. He wanted the screwdriver to force the lock or the doornails, not wanting to fire a gun but didn't think he could make himself touch it again. He walked slowly and dazedly over to the door, then fired a couple of bullets into the lock. It wasn't a deadbolt and came apart easily. If only it had been simpler, he thought. If only the old man could have lived. He sighed. He was thinking then that if he'd known how this trip was going to go, he'd never have attempted it. But that was pointless to consider. He couldn't undo any of it.

"After you, my good friend." Livingston gestured toward the door. He found that the simple phrase really did describe how he felt. Yes, this man was now a good friend. After everything they had just been through, Livingston knew that Wylie was the only person who would understand the emotions and consequences completely from their shared experiences.

Wylie managed a weak smile. "Thanks."

For some reason, he was hesitant. He walked slowly up the stairs and to the front door, then opened it, gazing for the first time in days at the night sky above. He hadn't realized how much he'd missed it and was overcome with emotion. Livingston came up behind him and patted the man on his back. The two of them would be bonded for life after this experience, lifelong friends, and he knew it.

Seeing the outside world wasn't as joyful as he'd wanted it to be, however. He felt as if they'd failed somehow. They didn't get the interview or their greatest questions answered, and the man would never be able to give answers again. Despite his madness, Lift was just an old man who decided, when it was too late, that he didn't want to be alone. It all evoked a sense of pity in Livingston, who knew he'd be seeing Lift in his nightmares for years to come.

Wylie looked over at Livingston,

not knowing what to say to signal his gratefulness to be alive, his thanks to Livingston for saving his life. Livingston was sad and happy at the same time, and he sighed again, gazing at the stars.

"Let's go home," Wylie said. "I'm ready to camp out under the stars tonight." He hadn't enjoyed the journey there, but he wanted to enjoy the journey home. He hoped Livingston wasn't injured too badly, and he looked at the man's leg. "Is that okay?"

Livingston nodded. "Just a flesh wound."

"We'll need to bandage it later. But now, let's get going."

Livingston felt tears beginning in the corners of his eyes as he felt his claustrophobia drift away. He felt a few come down his face, like a shock of disbelief that it was over. "Yes. Let's get going."

He was too frightened to go back down to collect the camping gear and their belongings, so Wylie had to go back down and bring it up in a few trips, saving the professor from facing his fears again. Then the two men began edging their way around the tower and around the cliff, facing a world of challenges ahead of them but feeling that the horrors of the past few days were behind them.

They set up a camp near the tower, and Wylie bandaged Livingston's leg, hoping he had done an adequate job. Then both men tried to sleep, still having nightmares that they were trapped. However, when they awoke, they could see the sky and clouds and heard birds overhead. They stood, breaking camp, and packed their belongings once again. Wylie stood near the edge of the cliff, looking out toward the horizon. And the sun shone brightly on the plain like

Cheryl Peña

someplace midnight never knew.

Cheryl Peña was born with her twin sister in San Antonio, Texas, in 1971. She learned to read and write at age four and began writing fiction and poetry shortly after. In 2000, she received an honors B.F.A. from the University of Texas-San Antonio, where she won an honorable mention in the juried student art show, upper-division, for her untitled photograph. She worked as a professional photographer for two years before beginning work as a legal secretary for a law firm. Upon the death of her twin sister in 2014, she decided to write professionally in her sister's honor. Her novella, *The House of Wynne Lift*, was first published in the October 2020 issue of the Scarlet Leaf Review. She still lives in San Antonio, Texas.

Made in the USA
Middletown, DE
14 August 2021